www.mascotbooks.com

For more information, please contact:
Mascot Books
560 Herndon Parkway #120
Herndon, VA 20170
info@mascotbooks.com

CPSIA Code: PRT0913A
ISBN-10: 1620862905
ISBN-13: 9781620862902

Printed in the United States

THAT'S NOT OUR MASCOT?
Big Al is Our Mascot

by Jason Wells and Jeff Wells
illustrated by Patrick Carlson

Who's that tailgating on the Quad?

That's not our mascot...
it's Big Red, the Arkansas Razorback.

Who's that playing in
the Million Dollar Band?

That's not our mascot...
it's Aubie, the Auburn Tiger.

Who's that shooting hoops
in Coleman Coliseum?

Who's that batting in
Sewell-Thomas Stadium?

That's not our mascot...
it's Hairy Dawg,
the Georgia Bulldog.

Who's that singing
"Yea, Alabama"?

Who's that eating at the Ferguson Center?

That's not our mascot...
it's Rebel, the Ole Miss Black Bear.

Who's that working out at the Rec Center?

Who's that touring the Bryant Museum?

Who's that strolling by the President's Mansion?

That's not our mascot....
it's Cocky, the South Carolina Gamecock.

Who's that studying at the Gorgas Library?

That's not our mascot...
it's Smokey, the Tennessee Volunteer.

Who's that looking up at Denny Chimes?

That's not our mascot...
it's Mr. C, the Vanderbilt® Commodore.

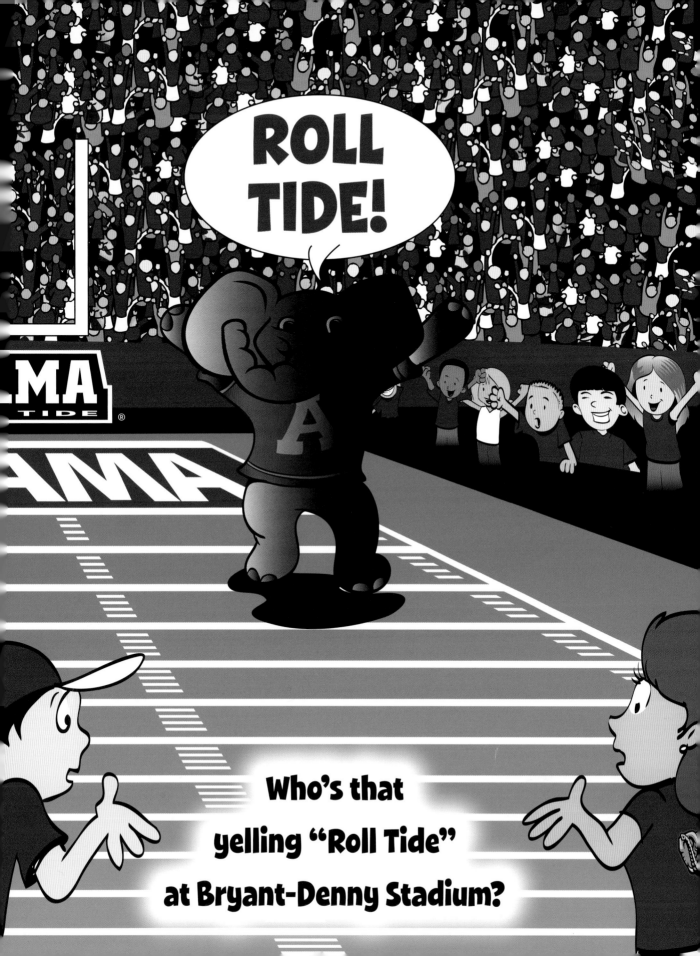

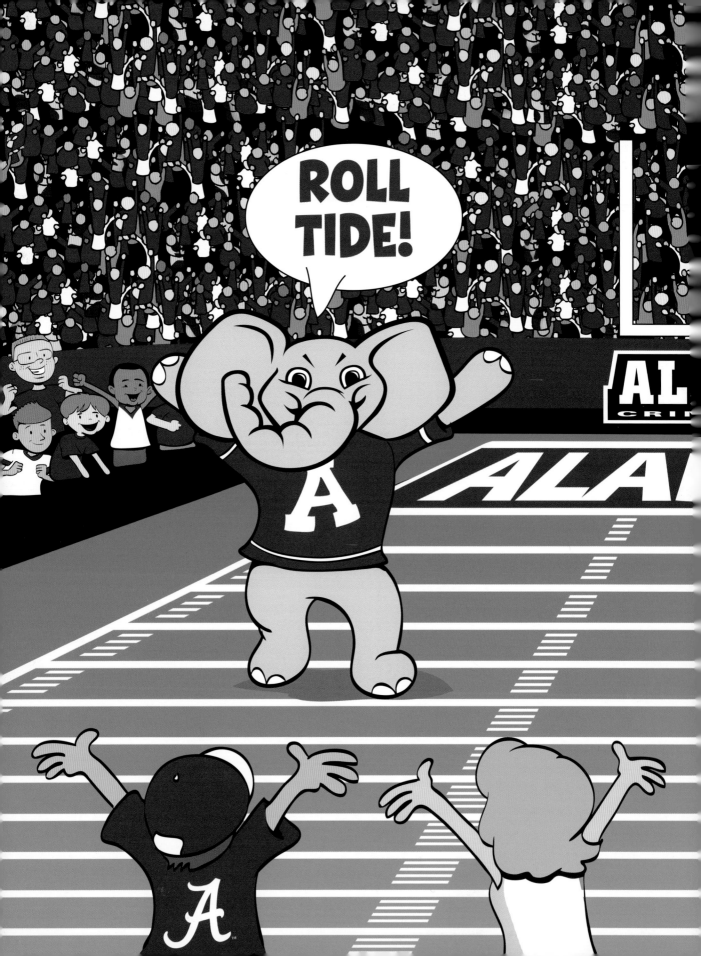